The Little Woods Runner

By Colleen Barksdale

Illustrated by
Andra Guzzo

The Little Woods Runner
by Colleen Barksdale

Printed in the United States of America

ISBN 9781498488648

www.xulonpress.com

Dedicated to our grandchildren
Dajahnae, DeNae, Dominica, Markell
Love from Granny CoCo and Gramps

Special thanks to
Christine Roiland and Jan Stefan-Friberg
for expertise and emotional support.

There once was a little girl
who loved to run in the woods.

In the springtime Dajahnae would come
to stay with her *special* Gramps
all day.

"What would you like to do?"
Gramps would say.
"Run in the woods all day and play,"
said little Dajahnae.

STOMP, STOMP, STOMP,
trip, slip, need to grip… on a tree.
Oh gee, we're having fun,
just Gramps and ME!

The summer came and
the woods grew thick.
No more walking because
of the ticks.

Sad was Little Woods
Runner's heart
because from the woods
she had to part.

Then one day Granny CoCo awoke with a start.
She had an idea in her mind and in her heart:
Blaze a trail, wide enough for a cart,
then Dajah can run from morning till dark...

Without Gramps, her dream trail
would not come true...

a path through the woods
so Little Woods Runner would not feel blue.

Granny CoCo was hopeful and confident in the plan because Gramps had every tool known to man.

An old pheasant pen, deep in the woods,
was blocking the plan to turn out like it should.
So Granny CoCo hacked, swiped, cut,
hauled, chopped and sawed.

The day came to show Dajah
the new wonders in the woods they had done…
so she, in the forest, could run.

Aunts and uncles, cousins
and great grandparents, too,
all came to see Dajah feel
proud as could be….

…because *her* trail was lined
with *her friends*, the TREES.

CPSIA information can be obtained
at www.ICGtesting.com
Printed in the USA
LVIC04n2227021216
515596LV00001B/1